The Power of Light

THE POWER OF LIGHT

Eight Stories for Hanukkah by

Isaac Bashevis Singer

with illustrations by

Irene Lieblich

A Sunburst Book

Farrar · Straus · Giroux

Text copyright © 1980 by Isaac Bashevis Singer
Illustrations copyright © 1980 by Irene Lieblich
All rights reserved
Library of Congress catalog card number: 80-20263
Published in Canada by HarperCollins*CanadaLtd*
Printed in the United States of America
First edition, 1980
Sunburst edition, 1990
Third printing, 1993

Contents

A Hanukkah Evening in My Parents' House

All year round my father, a rabbi in Warsaw, did not allow his children to play any games. Even when I wanted to play cat's cradle with my younger brother, Moishe, Father would say, "Why lose time on such nonsense? Better to recite psalms."

Often when I got two pennies from my father and I told him that I wanted to buy chocolate, ice cream, or colored pencils he would say, "You would do a lot better to find a poor man and give your pennies to him, because charity is a great deed."

But on Hanukkah, after Father lit the Hanukkah candles, he allowed us to play dreidel for half an hour. I remember one such night especially. It was the eighth night and in our Hanukkah lamp eight wicks were burning. Outside, a heavy snow had fallen. Even though our stove was hot, frost trees were forming on the windowpanes. My brother Joshua, who was eleven years older than I, already a grownup, was saying to my sister, Hindel, "Do you see the snow? Each flake is a hexagon; it has six sides with fancy little designs and decora-

tions—every one a perfect jewel and slightly different from all the others."

My brother Joshua read scientific books. He also painted landscapes—peasants' huts, fields, forests, animals, sometimes a sunset. He was tall and blond. Father wanted him to become a rabbi, but Joshua's ambition was to be an artist. My sister, Hindel, was even older than Joshua and already engaged to be married. She had dark hair and blue eyes. The idea that Hindel was going to be the wife of some strange young man and even going to change her surname seemed to me so peculiar that I refused to think about it.

When Father heard what Joshua had said about the snow, he promptly said, "It's all the work of God almighty, who bestows beauty on everything He creates."

"Why must each flake of snow be so beautiful, since people step on it or it turns to water?" Hindel asked.

"Everything comes easily to nature," Joshua answered. "The crystals arrange themselves in certain patterns. Take the frost trees—every winter they are the same. They actually look like fig trees and date trees."

"Such trees don't grow here in Poland but in the Holy Land," Father added. "When the Messiah comes, all God-fearing people will return to the land of Israel. There will be the resurrection of the dead. The Holy Temple will be rebuilt. The world will be as full of wisdom as the sea of water."

The door opened and Mother came in from the kitchen. She was frying the Hanukkah pancakes. Her lean face was flushed. For a while she stood there and listened. Although Mother was the daughter of a rabbi herself, she always pleaded with Father to be lenient and not to preach to us all the time as she felt he did. I heard her say, "Let the children have some fun. Who is winning?"

A Hanukkah Evening in My Parents' House

"It's little Moishe's lucky day," Hindel said. "He's cleaned us all out, the darling."

"Don't forget to give a few pennies to the poor," Father said to him. "In olden times one had to give tithe to the priests, but now the tithe should be given to the needy."

Mother nodded, smiled, and returned to the kitchen, and we continued our game. The tin dreidel, which I had bought before Hanukkah, had four Hebrew letters engraved on its sides: *nun, gimel, he,* and *shin.* According to Father, these letters were the initials of words which meant: a great miracle happened there—an allusion to the war between the Maccabees and the Greeks in 170 B.C. and the victory of the Maccabees. It is for this victory and the purification of the Holy Temple in Jerusalem from idols that Hanukkah is celebrated. But for us children *gimel* meant winning, *nun* losing, *he* half winning, and *shin* another chance for the player. Moishe and I took the game seriously, but Joshua and Hindel played only to keep us company. They always let us, the younger ones, win.

As for me, I was interested both in the game and in the conversation of the adults. As if he read my mind, I heard Joshua ask, "Why did God work miracles in ancient times and why doesn't He work miracles in our times?"

Father pulled at his red beard. His eyes expressed indignation.

"What are you saying, my son? God works miracles in all generations even though we are not always aware of them. Hanukkah especially is a feast of miracles. My grandmother Hindel—you, my daughter, are named after her—told me the following story. In the village of Tishewitz there was a child named Zaddock. He was a prodigy. When he was three years old, he could already read the Bible. At five he studied the

[7

Talmud. He was very goodhearted both to human beings and to animals. There was a mouse where his family lived and every day little Zaddock used to put a piece of cheese at the hole in the wall where the creature was hiding. At night he put a saucer of milk there. One day—it happened to be the third day of Hanukkah—little Zaddock overheard a neighbor tell of a sick tailor in the village who was so poor that he could not afford to buy wood to heat his hut. Little Zaddock had heard that in the forest near the village there were a lot of fallen branches to be picked up for nothing, and he decided to gather as much wood as he could carry and bring it to the sick man. The child was so eager to help that he immediately set out for the forest without telling his mother where he was going.

"It was already late in the day when he left the house, and by the time he reached the forest it was dark. Little Zaddock had lost his way and he would surely have died from the cold, when suddenly he saw in the darkness three Hanukkah lights. For a while they lingered before his eyes, and then they began to move slowly. Little Zaddock went after them, and they brought him back to the village, to the hut where the sick man lived with his family. When the lights reached the door of the sick man's hut, they fell, turning into gold coins. The sick man was able to buy bread for his family and himself, fuel to heat the oven, as well as oil for the Hanukkah lights. It wasn't long before he got well and was again able to earn a living."

"Daddy, what happened to Zaddock when he grew up?" I asked.

"He became a famous rabbi," Father said. "He was known as the saintly Rabbi Zaddock."

It became so quiet that I could hear the spluttering of the Hanukkah candles and the chirping of our house cricket.

Mother came in from the kitchen with two full plates of pancakes. They smelled delicious.

"Why is it so quiet—is the game over?" she asked.

My brother Moishe, who had seemed to be half asleep when Father told his story, suddenly opened his big blue eyes wide and said, "Daddy, I want to give the money I won to a sick tailor."

"You were preaching to them, huh?" Mother asked half reproachfully.

"I didn't preach, I told them a story," Father said. "I want them to know that what God could do two thousand years ago He can also do in our time."

The Extinguished

Lights

It was the custom to light the Hanukkah candles at home, rather than in a synagogue or studyhouse, but this particular studyhouse in Bilgoray was an exception. Old Reb Berish practically lived there. He prayed, studied the Mishnah, ate, and sometimes even slept on the bench near the stove. He was the oldest man in town. He admitted to being over ninety, but some maintained that he was already past one hundred. He remembered the war between Russia and Hungary. On holidays he used to visit Rabbi Chazkele from Kuzmir and other ancient rabbis.

That winter it snowed in Bilgoray almost every day. At night the houses on Bridge Street were snowed under and the people had to dig themselves out in the morning. Reb Berish had his own copper Hanukkah lamp, which the beadle kept in the reading table with other holy objects—a ram's horn, the Book of Esther written on a scroll, a braided Havdalah candle, a prayer shawl and phylacteries, as well as a wine goblet and an incense holder.

There is no moon on the first nights of Hanukkah, but that night the light from the stars made the snow sparkle as if it were full of diamonds. Reb Berish placed his Hanukkah lamp at the window according to the law, poured oil into the container, put a wick into it, and made the customary benedictions. Then he sat by the open clay stove. Even though most of the children stayed at home on Hanukkah evenings, a few boys came to the studyhouse especially to listen to Reb Berish's stories. He was known as a storyteller. While he told stories he roasted potatoes on the glowing coals. He was saying, "Nowadays when snow falls and there is a frost, people call it winter. In comparison to the winters of my times the winters of today are nothing. It used to be so cold that oak trees burst in the forests. The snow was up to the rooftops. Bevies of hungry wolves came into the village at night, and people shuddered in bed from their howling. The horses neighed in their stables and tried to break the doors open from fear. The dogs barked like mad. Bilgoray was still a tiny place then. There was a pasture where Bagno Street is today.

"The winter I'm going to tell you about was the worst of them all. The days were almost as dark as night. The clouds were black as lead. A woman would come out of her kitchen with the slop pail and the water turned to ice before she could empty it.

"Now hear something. That year the men blessed the Hanukkah lights on the first night as they did every year, but suddenly a wind came from nowhere and extinguished them. It happened in every house at the same time. The lights were kindled a second time, but again they were extinguished. In those times there was an abundance of wood to help keep the houses warm. To keep the wind out, cracks in the windows were plugged up with cotton or straw. So how could the wind get in? And why should it happen in every house at the same moment? Everybody was astonished. People went to the rabbi to ask his advice and the rabbi's decision was to continue rekindling the lights. Some pious men kept lighting the candles until the rooster crowed. This happened on the first night of Hanukkah, as well as on the second night and on the nights after. There were non-believers who contended that the whole thing was a natural occurrence. But most of the people believed that there was some mysterious power behind it all. But what was it—a demon, a mocker, an imp? And why just on Hanukkah?

"A fear came over the town. Old women said that it was an omen of war or an epidemic. Fathers and grandfathers were so disturbed that they forgot to give Hanukkah money to the children, who couldn't play games with the dreidel. The women did not fry pancakes as they had in former years.

"It went on like this until the seventh night. Then, after everyone was asleep and the rabbi was sitting in his chamber studying the Talmud, someone knocked on his door. It was the rabbi's custom to go to sleep early in the evening and to get up after midnight to study. Usually his wife served him tea, but in the middle of the night the rabbi poured water into the samovar himself, lit the coals, and prepared the tea. He would drink and study until daybreak.

"When the rabbi heard the knocking on the door, he got up and opened it. An old woman stood outside and the rabbi invited her to come into his house.

"She sat down and told the rabbi that last year before Hanukkah her little granddaughter Altele, an orphan, died. She had first gotten sick in the summer and no doctor could help her. After the High Holidays, when Altele realized that her end was near, she said, 'Grandmother, I know that I'm going to die, but I only wish to live until Hanukkah, when Grandpa gives me Hanukkah money and I can play dreidel with the girls.' Everybody in Bilgoray prayed for the girl's recovery, but it so happened that she died just a day before

Hanukkah. For a whole year after her death her grandparents never saw her in their dreams. But this night the grandmother had seen Altele in her dreams three times in a row. Altele came to her and said that because the people of the town had not prayed ardently enough for her to see the first Hanukkah candle, she had died angry and it was she who extinguished the Hanukkah lights in every house. The old woman said that after the first dream she awakened her husband and told him, but he said that because she brooded so much about her grandchild, she had had this dream. The second time when Altele came to her in her dream, the grandmother asked Altele what the people of the town could do to bring peace to her soul. The girl began to answer, but the old woman woke up suddenly before she could understand what Altele was saying. Only in the third dream did the girl speak clearly, saying it was her wish that on the last night of Hanukkah all the people of Bilgoray, together with the rabbi and the elders, should come to her grave and light the Hanukkah candles there. They should bring all the children with them, eat pancakes and play dreidel on the frozen snow.

"When the rabbi heard these words, he began to tremble, and he said, 'It's all my fault. I didn't pray enough for that child.' He told the old woman to wait, poured some tea for her, and looked in the books to see if what the girl asked was in accordance with the law. Though he couldn't find a similar case in all the volumes of his library, the rabbi decided on his own that the wish of that grieved spirit should be granted. He told the old woman that on a cold and windy night there is very little chance for lights to burn outdoors. However, if the ghost of the girl could extinguish all the lights indoors, she might also have the power to do the opposite. The rabbi promised the old woman to pray with all his heart for success.

"Early in the morning, when the beadle came to the rabbi,

he asked him to take his wooden hammer and go from house to house, knock on shutters, and tell the people what they must do. Even though Hanukkah is a holiday, the rabbi had ordered the older people to fast until noon and ask forgiveness of the girl's sacred soul—and also pray that there should be no wind in the evening.

"All day long a fierce wind blew. Chimneys were blown off some roofs. The sky was overcast with dark clouds. Not only the unbelievers, but even some of the God-fearing men, doubted lights could stay lit in a storm like this. There were those who suspected that the old woman invented the dream, or that a demon came to her disguised as her late grandchild in order to scoff at the faithful and lead them astray. The town's healer, Nissan, who trimmed his beard and came to the synagogue only on the Sabbath, called the old woman a liar and warned that the little ones might catch terrible colds at the graveyard and get inflammation of the lungs. The blizzard seemed to become wilder from minute to minute. But suddenly, while the people were reciting the evening prayer, a change took place. The sky cleared, the wind subsided, and warm breezes wafted from the surrounding fields and forests. It was already the beginning of the month of Teveth and a new moon was seen surrounded with myriads of stars.

"Some of the unbelievers were so stunned they couldn't utter a word. Nissan, the healer, promised the rabbi that scissors would never touch his beard again and that he would come to pray every day of the week. Not only older children, but even the younger ones, were taken to the graveyard. Lights were kindled, blessings were recited, the women served the pancakes with jam that they had prepared. The children played dreidel on the frozen snow, which was as smooth as ice. A golden light shone over the little girl's grave, a sign that her soul enjoyed the Hanukkah celebration. Never before or after did the graveyard seem so festive as on that eighth night of Hanukkah. All the unbelievers did penance. Even the Gentiles heard of the miracle and acknowledged that God had not forsaken the Jews.

"The next day Mendel the scribe wrote down the whole event in the parchment Community Book, but the book was burned years later in the time of the First Fire."

"When did this happen?" one of the children asked.

Reb Berish clutched his beard, which had once been red, then turned white, and finally became yellowish from the snuff he used. He pondered for a while and said, "Not less than eighty years ago."

"And you remember it so clearly?"

"As if it took place yesterday."

The light in Reb Berish's Hanukkah lamp began to sputter and smoke. The studyhouse became full of shadows. With his bare fingers the old man pulled three potatoes out of the stove, broke off some pieces, and offered them to the children. He said, "The body dies, but the soul goes up to God and lives forever."

"What do all the souls do when they are with God?" one of the boys asked.

"They sit in Paradise on golden chairs with crowns on their heads and God teaches them the secrets of the Torah."

"God is a teacher?"

"Yes, God is a teacher, and all the good souls are his pupils," Reb Berish replied.

"How long will the souls go on learning?" a boy asked.

"Until the Messiah comes, and then there will be the resurrection of the dead," Reb Berish said. "But even then God will continue to teach in his eternal yeshiva, because the secrets of the Torah are deeper than the ocean, higher than Heaven, and more delightful than all the pleasures the body could ever enjoy."

The Parakeet Named

Dreidel

It happened about ten years ago in Brooklyn, New York. All day long a heavy snow was falling. Toward evening the sky cleared and a few stars appeared. A frost set in. It was the eighth day of Hanukkah, and my silver Hanukkah lamp stood on the windowsill with all candles burning. It was mirrored in the windowpane, and I imagined another lamp outside.

My wife, Esther, was frying potato pancakes. I sat with my son, David, at a table and played dreidel with him. Suddenly David cried out, "Papa, look!" And he pointed to the window.

I looked up and saw something that seemed unbelievable. Outside on the windowsill stood a yellow-green bird watching the candles. In a moment I understood what had happened. A parakeet had escaped from its home somewhere, had flown out into the cold street and landed on my windowsill, perhaps attracted by the light.

A parakeet is native to a warm climate, and it cannot stand the cold and frost for very long. I immediately took steps to save the bird from freezing. First I carried away the

Hanukkah lamp so that the bird would not burn itself when entering. Then I opened the window and with a quick wave of my hand shooed the parakeet inside. The whole thing took only a few seconds.

In the beginning the frightened bird flew from wall to wall. It hit itself against the ceiling and for a while hung from a crystal prism on the chandelier. David tried to calm it, "Don't be afraid, little bird, we are your friends." Presently the bird flew toward David and landed on his head, as though it had been trained and was accustomed to people. David began to dance and laugh with joy. My wife, in the kitchen, heard the noise and came out to see what had happened. When she saw the bird on David's head, she asked, "Where did you get a bird all of a sudden?"

"Mama, it just came to our window."

"To the window in the middle of the winter?"

"Papa saved its life."

The bird was not afraid of us. David lifted his hand to his forehead and the bird settled on his finger. Esther placed a saucer of millet and a dish of water on the table, and the parakeet ate and drank. It saw the dreidel and began to push it with its beak. David exclaimed, "Look, the bird plays dreidel."

David soon began to talk about buying a cage for the bird and also about giving it a name, but Esther and I reminded him that the bird was not ours. We would try to find the owners, who probably missed their pet and were worried about what had happened to it in the icy weather. David said, "Meanwhile, let's call it Dreidel."

That night Dreidel slept on a picture frame and woke us in the morning with its singing. The bird stood on the frame, its plumage brilliant in the purple light of the rising sun, shaking as in prayer, whistling, twittering, and talking all at

the same time. The parakeet must have belonged to a house where Yiddish was spoken, because we heard it say, *"Zeldele, geh schlofen"* (Zeldele, go to sleep), and these simple words uttered by the tiny creature filled us with wonder and delight.

The next day I posted a notice in the elevators of the neighborhood houses. It said that we had found a Yiddish-speaking parakeet. When a few days passed and no one called, I advertised in the newspaper for which I wrote, but a week went by and no one claimed the bird. Only then did Dreidel become ours. We bought a large cage with all the fittings and toys that a bird might want, but because Hanukkah is a festival of freedom, we resolved never to lock the cage. Dreidel was free to fly around the house whenever he pleased. (The man at the pet shop had told us that the bird was a male.)

Nine years passed and Dreidel remained with us. We became more attached to him from day to day. In our house Dreidel learned scores of Yiddish, English, and Hebrew words. David taught him to sing a Hanukkah song, and there was always a wooden dreidel in the cage for him to play with. When I wrote on my Yiddish typewriter, Dreidel would cling to the index finger of either my right or my left hand, jumping acrobatically with every letter I wrote. Esther often joked that Dreidel was helping me write and that he was entitled to half my earnings.

Our son, David, grew up and entered college. One winter night he went to a Hanukkah party. He told us that he would be home late, and Esther and I went to bed early. We had just fallen asleep when the telephone rang. It was David. As a rule he is a quiet and composed young man. This time he spoke so excitedly that we could barely understand what he was saying. It seemed that David had told the story of our parakeet to his fellow students at the party, and a girl named Zelda Rosen had exclaimed, "I am this Zeldele! We lost our parakeet nine years ago." Zelda and her parents lived not far from us, but they had never seen the notice in the newspaper or the ones posted in elevators. Zelda was now a student and a friend of David's. She had never visited us before, although our son often spoke about her to his mother.

We slept little that night. The next day Zelda and her parents came to see their long-lost pet. Zelda was a beautiful and gifted girl. David often took her to the theater and to museums. Not only did the Rosens recognize their bird, but the bird seemed to recognize his former owners. The Rosens used to call him Tsip-Tsip, and when the parakeet heard them say "Tsip-Tsip," he became flustered and started to fly from one member of the family to the other, screeching and flapping his wings. Both Zelda and her mother cried when they saw their beloved bird alive. The father stared silently. Then he said, "We have never forgotten our Tsip-Tsip."

I was ready to return the parakeet to his original owners, but Esther and David argued that they could never part with Dreidel. It was also not necessary because that day David and Zelda decided to get married after their graduation from college. So Dreidel is still with us, always eager to learn new words and new games. When David and Zelda marry, they will take Dreidel to their new home. Zelda has often said, "Dreidel was our matchmaker."

On Hanukkah he always gets a gift—a mirror, a ladder, a bathtub, a swing, or a jingle bell. He has even developed a taste for potato pancakes, as befits a parakeet named Dreidel.

Menashe and Rachel

The poorhouse in Lublin had a special room for children—orphans, sick ones, and cripples. Menashe and Rachel were brought up there. Both of them were orphans and blind. Rachel was born blind and Menashe became blind from smallpox when he was three years old. Every day a tutor came to teach the children prayers, as well as a chapter of the five books of Moses. The older ones also learned passages of the Talmud. Menashe was now barely nine years old, but already he was known as a prodigy. He knew twenty chapters of the Holy Book by heart. Rachel, who was eight years old, could recite "I Thank Thee" in the morning, the Shema before going to sleep, make benedictions over food, and she also remembered a few supplications in Yiddish.

On Hanukkah the tutor blessed the Hanukkah lights for the children, and every child got Hanukkah money and a dreidel from the poorhouse warden. Rich women brought them pancakes sprinkled with sugar and cinnamon.

Some of the charity women maintained that the two blind children should not spend too much time together. First of all, Menashe was already a half-grown boy and a scholar, and there was no sense in his playing around with a little girl. Second, it's better for blind children to associate with seeing ones, who can help them find their way in the eternal darkness in which they live. But Menashe and Rachel were so very deeply attached to each other that no one could keep them apart.

Menashe was not only good at studying the Torah but also talented with his hands. All the other children got tin dreidels for Hanukkah, but Menashe carved two wooden ones for Rachel and himself. When Menashe was telling stories, even the grownups came to listen. Not only Rachel, but all the children in the poorhouse were eager to hear his stories. Some his mother had told him when she was still alive. Others he invented. He was unusually deft. In the summer he went with the other children to the river and did handstands and somersaults in the water. In the winter when a lot of snow fell, Menashe, together with other children, built a snowman with two coals for eyes.

Menashe had black hair. His eyes used to be black, too, but now they had whitish cataracts. Rachel was known as a beauty. She had golden hair and eyes as blue as cornflowers. Those who knew her could not believe that such shining eyes could be blind.

The love between Menashe and Rachel was spoken of not only in the poorhouse but in the whole neighborhood. Both children said openly that when they grew up they would marry. Some of the inmates in the poorhouse called them bride and groom. There were some do-gooders who believed the two children should be parted by force, but Rachel said that if she was taken away from Menashe she would drown herself in a well. Menashe warned that he would bite the hand that tried to separate him from Rachel. The poorhouse warden went to

ask the advice of the Lublin rabbi, and the rabbi said that the children should be left in peace.

One Hanukkah evening the children got their Hanukkah money and ate the tasty pancakes; then they sat down and played dreidel. It was the sixth night of Hanukkah. Six lights burned in the brass lamp in the window. Until tonight Menashe and Rachel had played together with the other children. But tonight Menashe said to Rachel, "Rachel, I have no desire to play."

"Neither have I," Rachel answered. "But what shall we do?"

"Let's sit down near the Hanukkah lamp and just be together."

Menashe led Rachel to the Hanukkah lamp. They followed the sweet smell of the oil in which the wicks were burning. They sat down on a bench. For a while both of them were silently enjoying each other's company as well as the warmth that radiated from the little flames. Then Rachel said, "Menashe, tell me a story."

"Again? I have told you all my stories already."

"Make up a new one," Rachel said.

"If I tell you all my stories now, what will I do when we marry and become husband and wife? I must save some stories for our future."

"Don't worry. By then you will have many new stories."

"Do you know what?" Menashe proposed. "You tell me a story this time."

"I have no story," Rachel said.

"How do you know that you don't have any? Just say whatever comes to your mind. This is what I do. When I'm asked to tell a story I begin to talk, not knowing what will come out. But somehow a story crops up by itself."

"With me nothing will crop up."

"Try."

"You will laugh at me."

"No, Rachel, I won't laugh."

It grew quiet. One could hear the wood burning in the clay stove. Rachel seemed to hesitate. She wet her lips with the tip of her tongue. Then she began, "Once there was a boy and a girl—"

"Aha."

"He was called Menashe and she Rachel."

"Yes."

"Everyone thought that Menashe and Rachel were blind, but they saw. I know for sure that Rachel saw."

"What did she see?" Menashe asked in astonishment.

"Other children see from the outside, but Rachel saw from the inside. Because of this people called her blind. It wasn't true. When people sleep, their eyes are closed, but in their dreams they can see boys, girls, horses, trees, goats, birds. So it was with Rachel. She saw everything deep in her head, many beautiful things."

"Could she see colors?" Menashe asked.

"Yes, green, blue, yellow, and other colors, I don't know what to call them. Sometimes they jumped around and formed little figures, dolls, flowers. Once, she saw an angel with six wings. He flew up high and the sky opened its golden doors for him."

"Could she see the Hanukkah lights?" Menashe asked.

"Not the ones from the outside, but those in her head. Don't you see anything, Menashe?"

"I, too, see things inside me," Menashe said after a long pause. "I see my father and my mother and also my grandparents. I never told you this, but I remember things from the time I could still see."

"What do you remember?" Rachel asked.

"Oh, I was sick and the room was full of sunshine. A doctor came, a tall man in a high hat. He told mother to pull down the curtain because he thought I was sick with the measles and it is not good when there is too much light in the room if you have measles."

"Why didn't you tell me this before?" Rachel asked.

"I thought you wouldn't understand."

"Menashe, I understand everything. Sometimes when I lie in bed at night and cannot fall asleep, I see faces and animals and children dancing in a circle. I see mountains, fields, rivers, gardens, and the moon shining over them."

"How does the moon look?"

"Like a face with eyes and a nose and a mouth."

"True. I remember the moon," Menashe said. "Sometimes at night when I lie awake I see many, many things and I don't know whether they are real or I'm only imagining. Once I saw a giant so tall his head reached the clouds. He had huge horns and a nose as big as the trunk of an elephant. He walked in the sea but the water only reached to his knees. I tried to tell the warden what I saw and he said I was lying. But I was telling the truth."

For some time both children were silent. Then Menashe said, "Rachel, as long as we are small we should never tell these secrets to anybody. People wouldn't believe us. They might think we were making them up. But when we grow up we will tell. It is written in the Bible, 'For the Lord seeth not as man seeth; for man looketh on the outward appearance but the Lord looketh on the heart.'"

"Who said this?"

"The prophet Samuel."

"Oh, Menashe, I wish we could grow up quickly and become husband and wife," Rachel said. "We will have children that see both from the outside and from the inside.

[*37*

You will kindle Hanukkah lights and I will fry pancakes. You will carve dreidels for our children to play with, and when they go to bed we will tell them stories. Later, when they fall asleep, they will dream about these stories."

"We will dream also," Menashe said. "I about you and you about me."

"Oh, I dream about you all the time. I see you in my dreams so clearly—your white skin, chiseled nose, black hair, beautiful eyes."

"I see you too—a golden girl."

Again there was silence. Then Rachel said, "I'd like to ask you something, but I am ashamed to say it."

"What is it?"

"Give me a kiss."

"Are you crazy? It's not allowed. Besides, when a boy kisses a girl they call him a sissy."

"No one will see."

"God sees," Menashe said.

"You said before that God looks into the heart. In my heart we are already grown up and I am your wife."

"The other children are going to laugh at us."

"They are busy with the dreidels. Kiss me! Just once."

Menashe took Rachel's hand and kissed her quickly. His heart was beating like a little hammer. She kissed him back and both of their faces were hot. After a while Menashe said, "It cannot be such a terrible sin, because it is written in the book of Genesis that Jacob loved Rachel and he kissed her when they met. Your name is Rachel, too."

The poorhouse warden came over. "Children, why are you sitting alone?"

"Menashe has just told me a story," Rachel answered.

"It's not true, she told me a story," Menashe said.

"Was it a nice story?" the warden asked.

"The most beautiful story in the whole world," Rachel said.

"What was it about?" the warden asked, and Menashe said, "About an island far away in the ocean full of lions, leopards, monkeys, as well as eagles and pheasants with golden feathers and silver beaks. There were many trees on the island —fig trees, date trees, pomegranate trees, and a stream with fresh water. There was a boy and a girl there who saved themselves from a shipwreck by clinging to a log. They were like Adam and Eve in Paradise, but there was no serpent and—"

"The children are fighting over the dreidel. Let me see what's going on," the warden said. "You can tell me the rest of the story tomorrow." He rushed to the table.

"Oh, you made up a new story," Rachel said. "What happened next?"

"They loved one another and got married," Menashe said.

"Alone on the island forever?" Rachel asked.

"Why alone?" Menashe said. "They had many children, six boys and six girls. Besides, one day a sailboat landed there and the whole family was rescued and taken to the land of Israel."

The Squire

Five Hanukkah lights burned in the Hanukkah lamp in the Trisker Hasidic studyhouse, as well as the large candle called the beadle. In the oven, potatoes were roasting and their smell tickled everyone's nostrils. Old Reb Berish sneezed and the boys around him wished him good health.

He wiped his nose with a large handkerchief and said, "Some people think that in olden times miracles were more frequent than today. That is not true. The truth is that miracles were rare in all times. If too many miracles occurred, people would rely on them too much. Free choice would cease. The Powers on High want men to do things, make an effort, not to be lazy. But there are cases where only a miracle can save a man.

"Something like this happened when I was a boy here in Bilgoray about eighty years ago—and perhaps even a little longer. Our village was much smaller than it is today. Where Zamość Street is now there was still forest. Lublin Street was only an alley. Where we are sitting now there was a pasture for cows. There lived then in Bilgoray a wealthy young man by the name of Falik, a Talmudic scholar. He was the owner of a dry-goods store. He had other businesses as well. His wife, Sarah, came from Lublin, from a fine family. Suddenly the couple's good luck changed. Whether it was a punishment for some transgression or just a decree from Heaven, I don't know. First, the store burned down. There was no fire insurance in those years. Then Sarah became ill. There was no doctor or druggist in Bilgoray. There were only three remedies for people to apply—leeches, cups, and bleeding. If these three didn't help, nothing more could be done. Sarah died and left three orphans, a boy by the name of Mannes and two younger girls, Pessele and Etele.

"Not long after Sarah's death, Falik himself became mortally sick. He grew pale and emaciated, and after a while he became bedridden and it seemed he would never recover. Lippe the healer recommended chicken broth, barley soup, and goat milk. Nothing changed. First of all, Falik lost his appetite, and second, he was left without any income. Nowadays people are selfish, they don't care about others, but in former times people helped one another when in need. They tried to send bread to Falik and meat, butter, and cheese, but he refused to accept charity. The community leader came to him and offered him help secretly, so that no one would know, but Falik said, 'I would know.'

"It happened the first night of Hanukkah. As always there was a great deal of snow, frost, blizzards. Things had reached such a stage in Falik's house that finally there was not even a loaf of bread. In better times Falik had possessed a number of silver objects—candlesticks, a spice box, a Passover plate—but Mannes, the oldest child, had sold them all. There was one precious article still in the house, an antique Hanukkah lamp made by some ancient silversmith. There lived a usurer in town who would pay a pittance for the most costly objects. Mannes wanted to sell him the Hanukkah lamp, too, but

Falik said to his son, 'Wait until after Hanukkah.' There were a few pennies left in the house, but instead of buying bread Mannes bought oil and wicks for the Hanukkah lights. The girls complained that they were hungry, and Mannes said to them, 'Let's imagine that it is Yom Kippur.' I know this story, because Mannes told it to me years later.

"Since Falik could not leave bed any more, Mannes brought the lamp to his father on the first night of Hanukkah and Falik made the proper benedictions and lit the first light. He also hummed the song 'Rock of Ages,' and kissed his children. Then Mannes took the Hanukkah lamp to the living room and put it on the windowsill, according to the law. The children sat at the table hungry, without having eaten supper. It was cold in the house. Only a year before, Falik had given his children Hanukkah money to play dreidel and Sarah had fried pancakes for the family. Now everything was bathed in gloom. The children looked at each other with eyes that seemed to ask, 'From whence cometh my help?'

"Suddenly someone knocked at the door. 'Who could this be?' Mannes asked himself. 'Probably someone with a gift.' His father had warned him again and again not to accept any gifts. Mannes decided not to open the door this time, so as to avoid arguing with the good people. But the knocking at the door did not stop. After a while Mannes went to the door, ready to say, 'Father told me not to accept anything.' When he opened it he saw a squire—tall, broad-shouldered, in a long fur coat with tails down to his ankles and a fur hat sprinkled with snow. Mannes became so frightened that he lost his tongue. It almost never happened that a squire came into a Jewish house, especially in the evening. In my day, when a squire visited a village, he came in a carriage harnessed to eight horses, and his valets rode in front to clear a way for him. Often they blew trumpets to announce that the great lord was coming. Bilgoray still belonged to Count Zamojski, who was as rich and mighty as a king. To Mannes the squire said, 'I passed by in my sleigh and I saw a little light in a lamp the likes of which I had never seen in all my life—with goblets, flowers, a lion, a deer, a leopard, an eagle, all beautifully done. Why did you kindle only one light if there are eight holders? Is this some Jewish holiday? And where are your parents?' Mannes knew Polish and how to speak to an important man. He said, 'Come in, your excellency. It is for us a great honor.'

"The squire entered the living room and for a long while he stared at the Hanukkah lamp. He began to question Mannes, and the boy told him the story of Hanukkah—how the Jews fought the Greeks in ancient times in the land of Israel. He also told him of the miracle that had happened with the oil for lighting the menorah in the temple: how after the war there was barely enough oil left to light the menorah for one day, but a miracle happened and the oil was sufficient for eight days. Then the squire saw a dreidel on the table and asked, 'What is this?'

"Although the children had no money with which to play, they had put a dreidel there just to remember former times. Mannes explained to the squire that Hanukkah is the only holiday when children are allowed to play games. He told him the rules of dreidel. The squire asked, 'Could I play with you? My driver will wait with the sleigh. It's cold outside, but my horses are covered with blankets and the driver has a fur jacket.'

" 'Your excellency,' Mannes said, 'my father is sick. We have no mother and we don't have a penny to our name.' The squire said, 'I intend to offer you a thousand gulden for your magnificent lamp, but I don't have the whole sum with me, so I will give you five hundred gulden in advance and with this money you can play.' As he said this, he took a large bag

of gold coins from his coat and threw it on the table. The children were so astounded that they forgot their hunger. The game began and the greatest unbeliever could have seen that the whole event was a wonder from Heaven. The children kept winning and the squire kept losing. In one hour the squire lost all his gold and the children won every coin. Then the squire cried out, 'Lost is lost. My driver and my horses must be cold. Good night, happy Hanukkah, and don't worry about your father. With God's help he will soon recover.'

"Only after the squire had left did the children realize what had happened to them. Not only had they gotten five hundred gulden as an advance on the lamp, but the squire had lost additional money. Half the table was covered with coins. The girls, Pessele and Etele, burst out crying. Mannes ran outside to see if the squire, the sleigh, the horses and driver were still there, but they had all vanished without leaving any tracks in the snow. Usually horses harnessed to a sleigh have bells on their necks and one can hear the jingling from far away, but the night was quiet. I will make it short. The moment the squire left, Falik opened his eyes. He had gone to sleep near to death and he woke up a healthy man. Nothing but a miracle could have saved him, and so the miracle occurred."

"Who was the squire? The prophet Elijah?" the boys asked.

"Who knows? He certainly was not a Polish squire."

"Did he ever come to get the lamp?"

"Not as long as I was in Bilgoray," the old man replied.

"If he had been the prophet Elijah, he would have kept his promise," one of the boys remarked.

Old Reb Berish did not answer immediately. He pulled his beard and pondered. Then he said, "They have a lot of time in Heaven. He might have come to their children's children or to their grandchildren. I married and moved to another village. As far as I know the Hanukkah lamp remained with Falik and his children as long as they lived. Some rabbi said that when God works a miracle, He often does it in such a way that it should appear natural. There were some unbelievers in Bilgoray and they said that it was a real squire, a rich spendthrift who was in a mood to squander his money. Those who deny God always try to explain all wonders as normal events or as coincidences—I'm afraid the potatoes are already burning," he added.

Old Reb Berish opened the door of the oven and with his bare fingers began to pull out half-burned potatoes from the glowing coals.

The Power of Light

During World War II, after the Nazis had bombed and burned the Warsaw ghetto, a boy and a girl were hiding in one of the ruins—David, fourteen years old, and Rebecca, thirteen.

It was winter and bitter cold outside. For weeks Rebecca had not left the dark, partially collapsed cellar that was their hiding place, but every few days David would go out to search for food. All the stores had been destroyed in the bombing, and David sometimes found stale bread, cans of food, or whatever else had been buried. Making his way through the ruins was dangerous. Sometimes bricks and mortar would fall down, and he could easily lose his way. But if he and Rebecca did not want to die from hunger, he had to take the risk.

That day was one of the coldest. Rebecca sat on the ground wrapped in all the garments she possessed; still, she could not get warm. David had left many hours before, and Rebecca listened in the darkness for the sound of his return, knowing that if he did not come back nothing remained to her but death.

Suddenly she heard heavy breathing and the sound of a

bundle being dropped. David had made his way home. Rebecca could not help but cry "David!"

"Rebecca!"

In the darkness they embraced and kissed. Then David said, "Rebecca, I found a treasure."

"What kind of treasure?"

"Cheese, potatoes, dried mushrooms, and a package of candy—and I have another surprise for you."

"What surprise?"

"Later."

Both were too hungry for a long talk. Ravenously they ate the frozen potatoes, the mushrooms, and part of the cheese. They each had one piece of candy. Then Rebecca asked, "What is it now, day or night?"

"I think night has fallen," David replied. He had a wristwatch and kept track of day and night and also of the days of the week and the month. After a while Rebecca asked again, "What is the surprise?"

"Rebecca, today is the first day of Hanukkah, and I found a candle and some matches."

"Hanukkah tonight?"

"Yes."

"Oh, my God!"

"I am going to bless the Hanukkah candle," David said.

He lit a match and there was light. Rebecca and David stared at their hiding place—bricks, pipes, and the uneven ground. He lighted the candle. Rebecca blinked her eyes. For the first time in weeks she really saw David. His hair was matted and his face streaked with dirt, but his eyes shone with joy. In spite of the starvation and persecution David had grown taller, and he seemed older than his age and manly. Young as they both were, they had decided to marry if they could manage to escape from war-ridden Warsaw. As a token of their engagement, David had given Rebecca a shiny groschen he found in his pocket on the day when the building where both of them lived was bombed.

Now David pronounced the benediction over the Hanukkah candle, and Rebecca said, "Amen." They had both lost their families, and they had good reason to be angry with God for sending them so many afflictions, but the light of the candle brought peace into their souls. That glimmer of light, surrounded by so many shadows, seemed to say without words: Evil has not yet taken complete dominion. A spark of hope is still left.

For some time David and Rebecca had thought about escaping from Warsaw. But how? The ghetto was watched by the Nazis day and night. Each step was dangerous. Rebecca kept delaying their departure. It would be easier in the summer, she often said, but David knew that in their predicament they had little chance of lasting until then. Somewhere in the forest there were young men and women called partisans who fought the Nazi invaders. David wanted to reach them. Now, by the light of the Hanukkah candle, Rebecca suddenly felt renewed courage. She said, "David, let's leave."

"When?"

"When you think it's the right time," she answered.

"The right time is now," David said. "I have a plan."

For a long time David explained the details of his plan to Rebecca. It was more than risky. The Nazis had enclosed the ghetto with barbed wire and posted guards armed with machine guns on the surrounding roofs. At night searchlights lit up all possible exits from the destroyed ghetto. But in his wanderings through the ruins, David had found an opening to a sewer which he thought might lead to the other side. David told Rebecca that their chances of remaining alive were slim. They could drown in the dirty water or freeze to death. Also, the sewers were full of hungry rats. But Rebecca agreed to take the risk; to remain in the cellar for the winter would mean certain death.

When the Hanukkah light began to sputter and flicker before going out, David and Rebecca gathered their few belongings. She packed the remaining food in a kerchief, and David took his matches and a piece of lead pipe for a weapon.

In moments of great danger people become unusually courageous. David and Rebecca were soon on their way through the ruins. They came to passages so narrow they had to crawl on hands and knees. But the food they had eaten, and the joy the Hanukkah candle had awakened in them, gave them the courage to continue. After some time David found the entrance to the sewer. Luckily the sewage had frozen, and it seemed that the rats had left because of the extreme cold. From time to time David and Rebecca stopped to rest and to listen. After a while they crawled on, slowly and carefully. Suddenly they stopped in their tracks. From above they could hear the clanging of a trolley car. They had reached the other side of the ghetto. All they needed now was to find a way to get out of the sewer and to leave the city as quickly as possible.

Many miracles seemed to happen that Hanukkah night. Because the Nazis were afraid of enemy planes, they had ordered a complete blackout. Because of the bitter cold, there were fewer Gestapo guards. David and Rebecca managed to leave the sewer and steal out of the city without being caught. At dawn they reached a forest where they were able to rest and have a bite to eat.

Even though the partisans were not very far from Warsaw, it took David and Rebecca a week to reach them. They walked at night and hid during the days—sometimes in granaries and sometimes in barns. Some peasants stealthily helped the partisans and those who were running away from the Nazis. From time to time David and Rebecca got a piece of bread, a few potatoes, a radish, or whatever the peasants could spare. In one village they encountered a Jewish partisan who had come to get food for his group. He belonged to the Haganah, an organization that sent men from Israel to rescue Jewish refugees from the Nazis in occupied Poland. This young man brought David and Rebecca to the other partisans who roamed the forest. It was the last day of Hanukkah, and that evening the partisans lit eight candles. Some of them played dreidel on the stump of an oak tree while others kept watch.

From the day David and Rebecca met the partisans, their life became like a tale in a storybook. They joined more and more refugees who all had but one desire—to settle in the land of Israel. They did not always travel by train or bus. They walked. They slept in stables, in burned-out houses, and wherever they could hide from the enemy. To reach their destination, they had to cross Czechoslovakia, Hungary, and Yugoslavia. Somewhere at the seashore in Yugoslavia, in the middle of the night, a small boat manned by a Haganah crew waited for them, and all the refugees with their meager belongings were packed into it. This all happened silently and in great secrecy, because the Nazis occupied Yugoslavia.

But their dangers were far from over. Even though it was spring, the sea was stormy and the boat was too small for such a long trip. Nazi planes spied the boat and tried without success to sink it with bombs. They also feared the Nazi submarines which were lurking in the depths. There was nothing the refugees could do besides pray to God, and this time God seemed to hear their prayers, because they managed to land safely.

The Jews of Israel greeted them with a love that made them forget their suffering. They were the first refugees who

[59

had reached the Holy Land, and they were offered all the help and comfort that could be given. Rebecca and David found relatives in Israel who accepted them with open arms, and although they had become quite emaciated, they were basically healthy and recovered quickly. After some rest they were sent to a special school where foreigners were taught modern Hebrew. Both David and Rebecca were diligent students. After finishing high school, David was able to enter the academy of engineering in Haifa, and Rebecca, who excelled in languages and literature, studied in Tel Aviv—but they always met on weekends. When Rebecca was eighteen, she and David were married. They found a small house with a garden in Ramat Gan, a suburb of Tel Aviv.

I know all this because David and Rebecca told me their story on a Hanukkah evening in their house in Ramat Gan about eight years later. The Hanukkah candles were burning, and Rebecca was frying potato pancakes served with applesauce for all of us. David and I were playing dreidel with their little son, Menahem Eliezer, named after both of his grandfathers. David told me that this large wooden dreidel was the same one the partisans had played with on that Hanukkah evening in the forest in Poland. Rebecca said to me, "If it had not been for that little candle David brought to our hiding place, we wouldn't be sitting here today. That glimmer of light awakened in us a hope and strength we didn't know we possessed. We'll give the dreidel to Menahem Eliezer when he is old enough to understand what we went through and how miraculously we were saved."

Hershele and Hanukkah

Three lights burned in old Reb Berish's menorah. It was so quiet in the studyhouse one could hear the wick in the ceiling lamp sucking kerosene. Reb Berish was saying:

"Children, when one lives as long as I do, one sees many things and has many stories to tell. What I am going to tell you now happened in the village of Gorshkow.

"Gorshkow is small even today. But when I was a boy the marketplace was the entire village. They used to joke, 'Whenever a peasant comes with his cart to Gorshkow, the head of the horse is at one end of the village and the rear wheels of the cart at the other end.' Fields and forests surrounded Gorshkow on all sides. A man by the name of Isaac Seldes who lived there managed a huge estate owned by a Polish squire. The squire, a count, spent all his time abroad and came to Poland only when his money was exhausted. He borrowed more money from Reb Isaac Seldes on mortgage and gradually his whole estate became Isaac's property. Officially, it still belonged to the squire because a Jew was not allowed to own land in the part of Poland which belonged to Russia.

"Reb Isaac managed the property with skill. The squire

used to flog the peasants when they did something wrong or if the mood struck him. But Reb Isaac spoke to the peasants as if they were his equals and they were loyal to him. When there was a wedding among them or when a woman gave birth, he attended the celebration. When a peasant fell sick, Reb Isaac's wife, Kreindl, rolled up her sleeves and applied cups or leeches or rubbed the patient with turpentine. Reb Isaac Seldes owned a britska with two horses, and he rode alongside the fields and advised the peasants when to plow, what to sow, or what vegetables to plant. He had a special dairy house on the estate for churning butter and making cheese. He had a large stable for cows, hundreds of chickens that laid eggs, as well as beehives and a water mill.

"He had everything except children. It caused Reb Isaac and his wife grief. The medications that the doctors of Lublin prescribed for Kreindl never did any good.

"Even though they were only two people, Reb Isaac and his wife lived in a large house that had once belonged to the present squire's grandfather. But what use is a big house for just a husband and a wife? However, they both had poor relatives whose children came to live on the estate. Reb Isaac hired a teacher to instruct the boys in the Bible and the Talmud. Kreindl taught the girls sewing, knitting, and needle-point. They stitched Biblical scenes onto canvas with colored thread, like the story of Abraham attempting to sacrifice his only son on an altar and the angel preventing him from doing so, or Jacob meeting Rachel at the well and rolling the stone away so she could water the sheep.

"Hanukkah was always a gay occasion in Reb Isaac's house. After blessing the candles he gave Hanukkah money to all the children and they all played dreidel. Kreindl and her maids fried potato pancakes in the kitchen and they were served with jam and tea. Often poor people turned up at the estate, and whoever came hungry in tattered clothes and bare-foot left with a full belly, warm clothing, and proper footwear.

"One Hanukkah evening when the children were playing dreidel and Reb Isaac was playing chess with the teacher, who was not only a Talmud scholar but also well versed in mathematics and language, Reb Isaac heard a scratching at the door. A deep snow had fallen outside. If guests visited the estate in the winter, they came during the day, not in the evening. Reb Isaac opened the door himself, and to his amazement, on the other side of the threshold stood a fawn, still without antlers. Normally, an animal keeps away from human beings, but this fawn seemed hungry, cold, and emaciated. Perhaps it had lost its mother. For a while Reb Isaac stared in wonder. Then he took the young animal by its throat and brought it into the house. When the children saw the fawn, they forgot about the dreidel and the Hanukkah gifts. They were all thrilled with the charming animal. When she saw the fawn, Kreindl almost dropped the tray of pancakes she was holding. Reb Isaac wanted to give a pancake to the fawn, but Kreindl called out, 'Don't do it. It's too young. It needs milk, not pancakes.' The maids came in and one of them went to bring a bowl of milk. The fawn drank all of it and lifted up its head as if to say, 'I want more.' This little creature brought much joy to everybody in the house. All agreed that the fawn should not be let out again in the woods, which teemed with wolves, foxes, martens, and even bears. A servant brought in some hay and made a bed for the fawn in one of the rooms. Soon, it fell asleep.

"Reb Isaac thought that soon the children would return to their games, but all they could talk about was the fawn, and Reb Isaac and Kreindl had to give them a solemn promise to keep it safe in the house until after Passover.

"Now that the children had extracted this promise, a new

debate began—what name to give the fawn? Almost everyone wanted to call it Hershele, which is the Yiddish word for fawn, but for some strange reason Kreindl said, 'You are not going to give this name to the animal.'

" 'Why not?' the children and even the grownups asked in astonishment.

" 'I have a reason.'

"When Kreindl said no, it remained no. The children had to come up with another name, and then Kreindl said, 'Children, I have it.'

" 'What is it?' the children asked in unison. And Kreindl said 'Hanukkah.'

"No one had ever heard of an animal called Hanukkah, but they liked it. Only now did the children start to eat the pancakes, and they washed them down with tea with lemon and jam. Then they began to play dreidel again and they did not finish the games until midnight.

"Late at night, when Reb Isaac and Kreindl went to bed, Reb Isaac asked Kreindl, 'Why didn't you like the name Hershele for the fawn?' and Kreindl replied, 'That is a secret.'

" 'A secret from me?' Isaac asked. 'Since we married you've never had any secrets from me.'

"And Kreindl answered, 'This time I cannot tell you.'

" 'When will you tell me?' Isaac asked, and Kreindl said, 'The secret will reveal itself.'

"Reb Isaac had never heard his wife speak in riddles but it was not in his nature to insist or to probe.

"Now, dear children, I am going to tell you the secret even before Kreindl told it to her husband," old Reb Berish said.

"A few weeks earlier an old man came to the estate with a sack on his back and a cane in his hand. He had a white beard and white sidelocks. When Kreindl gave him food to eat he

took a large volume out of his sack, and while he ate, he read it. Kreindl had never seen a beggar behave like a rabbi and a scholar. She asked him, 'Why do you carry books on your back? Aren't they heavy?' And the old man replied, 'The Torah is never heavy.' His words impressed Kreindl so she began to talk to him and she told him how grieved she was at not having children. Suddenly she heard herself say, 'I see that you are a holy man. Please, pray to God for me and give me your blessing. I promise you that if your blessing is answered in Heaven, I will give you a sack full of silver guldens when you return and you will never need to beg for alms.'

" 'I promise you that in about a year's time you will have a child.'

" 'Please, holy man,' Kreindl said. 'Give me a token or a sign that your promise will come true.' And the old man said, 'Some time before your child is conceived an animal will enter your house. When the child is born, call it by the name of this animal. Please remember my words.'

"Before the old man left, Kreindl wanted to give him clothes and food, but he said, 'God will provide all this for me. I don't need to prepare it in advance. Besides, my sack is filled with sacred books and there is no place for anything else.' He lifted his hands over Kreindl's head and blessed her. Then he left as quietly as he had come. Kreindl pondered the words of this strange old man for many weeks. Reb Isaac happened not to be at home when he came and Kreindl did not tell her husband about his visit. She had received many wishes and benedictions from gypsies, fortune-tellers, and wanderers, and she did not want to arouse hopes in Isaac that might never materialize.

"That night when the fawn came into the house Kreindl understood that this was the animal the beggar had mentioned. Since a fawn is called Hershele in Yiddish, she would give birth to a male child and call him Hershele. Kreindl's words that the secret would reveal itself soon came true. She became pregnant and Reb Isaac understood that the coming of the fawn was an omen of this hoped-for event. He said, 'When our child is born, if it is a male we will call it Hershele,' and Kreindl answered, 'As you wish, my beloved, so it will be.'

"Winter had passed, spring had come. Hanukkah had been growing in the cold winter months and he sprouted antlers. Everyone could see that the animal was no longer happy indoors. His beautiful eyes expressed a yearning to go back to the forest. One morning Kreindl gave Hanukkah a tasty meal of hay mixed with chopped potatoes and carrots and then opened the gate to the fields and forests. Hanukkah gave his mistress a look that said 'Thank you,' and he ran to the green pastures and the woods.

"Kreindl predicted that in the winter Hanukkah would turn up again, but Reb Isaac said such things cannot be foretold. 'Hanukkah has grown up and an adult deer can find its own food even in the winter.'

"Not long after, Kreindl gave birth to a healthy little boy with dark hair and brown eyes and there was great joy in the house. The happy father and mother had prepared a special repast for the poor on the day of the circumcision ceremony. Reb Isaac and Kreindl both hoped that the old beggar might hear about it and come to the feast. But he never came. However, other poor people heard about it and they came. A large table was placed on the lawn and the needy men and women were served challah, gefilte fish, chicken, fruit, as well as wine and honey cake. Some of the younger crowd danced a scissor dance, a good-morning dance, an angry dance, a kazatske. Before they left, all the poor got gifts of money, food, and clothes.

"The summer drew to a close and it became cool again.

Hershele and Hanukkah

After the Succoth holiday the rains, the snowfall, and the frosts began. The feast of Hanukkah approached, and although everyone wondered what had happened to the fawn in the cold weather, nobody spoke about it, so as not to worry Kreindl. This winter was even more severe than the former one. The whole estate was buried in snow. On the first night of Hanukkah Kreindl and the maids were busy frying pancakes. After Reb Isaac blessed the first light and gave coins to the children, they sat down to play dreidel. The baby, Hershele, slept in his cradle. The children of the house had prepared a gift for him—a fawn made of sugar, and on its belly was the inscription 'Hanukkah.' When it was given to Hershele he immediately began to suck on it. But the fawn didn't come that night. Reb Isaac comforted Kreindl by quoting the Gemara: 'Miracles don't happen every day.'

"Kreindl shook her head. 'I hope to God that Hanukkah is not hungry and cold.'

"On the second night of Hanukkah, while all the children were playing dreidel, Reb Isaac was about to checkmate the teacher, and Kreindl, along with the maids, was preparing to clean the table, they heard a scratching on the door. Kreindl ran to open it and cried out with joy. At the door stood Hanukkah, already a half-grown deer, his body silvery with frost. He had not forgotten his benefactors. He had come to stay for the winter. Hershele woke up from the noise, and when he was shown the animal he stretched out his little hand toward him. Hanukkah licked the hand with his tongue, as if he knew that Hershele was his namesake.

"From then on, the deer came to the estate every year and always about the time of Hanukkah. He had become a big stag with large antlers. Hershele grew too, although not as fast. The third winter the deer brought a doe with him. It seemed that he had fought for his mate with another stag because a part of his antler was broken. Hanukkah and his mate were taken in. There was much discussion among the children what to name Hanukkah's wife. This time the teacher made a proposal. She was named Zot Hanukkah. This is how the section of the Bible that is read on the Sabbath of Hanukkah begins. The word 'Zot,' which means 'this,' indicates the feminine gender. This name pleased everyone."

Reb Berish paused for a long while. The lights in the brass lamp were still burning. The children felt that the little flames were also listening to the story. Then a boy asked, "Did the old beggar ever come back?"

"No, I never heard that he did, but you can be sure that this man was not just an ordinary beggar."

"What was he?" another boy asked.

"The prophet Elijah," Reb Berish said. "It is known that Elijah is the angel of good tidings. He never comes in the image of an angel. People would go blind if they looked into the dazzling light of an angel. He always comes disguised as a poor man. Even the Messiah, according to the Talmud, will come in the disguise of a poor man, riding on a donkey."

Old Reb Berish closed his eyes and it was hard to know whether he was dozing or contemplating the coming of the Messiah. He opened them again and said, "Now you can go home and play dreidel."

"Will you tell us another story tomorrow?" another boy asked, and old Reb Berish replied, "With God's help. I have lived long and I have more stories to tell than you have hair in your sidelocks."

Hanukkah

in the Poorhouse

Outside there was snow and frost, but in the poorhouse it was warm. Those who were mortally ill or paralyzed lay in beds. The others were sitting around a large Hanukkah lamp with eight burning wicks. Goodhearted citizens had sent pancakes sprinkled with sugar and cinnamon to the inmates. They conversed about olden times, unusual frosts, packs of wolves invading the villages during the icy nights, as well as encounters with demons, imps, and sprites. Among the paupers sat an old man, a stranger who had arrived only two days before. He was tall, straight, and had a milk-white beard. He didn't look older than seventy, but when the warden of the poorhouse asked him his age, he pondered a while, counted on his fingers, and said, "On Passover I will be ninety-two."

"No evil eye should befall you," the others called out in unison.

"When you live, you get older not younger," the old man said.

One could hear from his pronunciation that he was not from Poland but from Russia. For an hour or so he listened

[75

to the stories which the other people told, while looking intensely at the Hanukkah lights. The conversation turned to the harsh decrees against the Jews and the old man said, "What do you people in Poland know about harsh decrees? In comparison to Russia, Poland is Paradise."

"Are you from Russia?" someone asked him.

"Yes, from Vitebsk."

"What are you doing here?" another one asked.

"When you wander, you come to all kinds of places," the old man replied.

"You seem to speak in riddles," an old woman said.

"My life was one great riddle."

The warden of the poorhouse, who stood nearby, said, "I can see that this man has a story to tell."

"If you have the patience to listen," the old man said.

"Here we *must* have patience," the warden replied.

"It is a story about Hanukkah," said the old man. "Come closer, because I like to talk, not shout."

They all moved their stools closer and the old man began.

"First let me tell you my name. It is Jacob, but my parents called me Yankele. The Russians turned Yankele into Yasha. I mention the Russians because I am one of those who are called the captured ones. When I was a child Tsar Nicholas I, an enemy of the Jews, decreed that Jewish boys should be captured and brought up to be soldiers. The decree was aimed at Russian Jews, not at Polish ones. It created turmoil. The child catchers would barge into a house or into a cheder, where the boys studied, catch a boy as if he were some animal, and send him away deep into Russia, sometimes as far as Siberia. He was not drafted immediately. First he was given to a peasant in a village where he would grow up, and then, when he was of age, he was taken into the army. He had to learn Russian and forget his Jewishness. Often he was forced to convert to the Greek Orthodox faith. The peasant made him work on the Sabbath and eat pork. Many boys died from the bad treatment and from yearning for their parents.

"Since the law stipulated that no one who was married could be drafted for military service, the Jews often married little boys to little girls to save the youngsters from being captured. The married little boy continued to go to cheder. The little girl put on a matron's bonnet, but she remained a child. It often happened that the young wife went out in the street to play with pebbles or to make mud cakes. Sometimes she would take off her bonnet and put her toys in it.

"What happened to me was of a different nature. The young girl whom I was about to marry was the daughter of a neighbor. Her name was Reizel. When we were children of four or five, we played together. I was supposed to be her husband and she my wife. I made believe that I went to the synagogue and she prepared supper for me, a shard with sand or mud. I loved Reizel and we promised ourselves that when we grew up we really would become husband and wife. She was fair, with red hair and blue eyes. Some years later, when my parents brought me the good tidings that Reizel was to marry me, I became mad with joy. We would have married immediately; however, Reizel's mother insisted on preparing a trousseau for the eight-year-old bride, even though she would grow out of it in no time.

"Three days before our wedding, two Cossacks broke into our house in the middle of the night, tore me from my bed, and forced me to follow them. My mother fainted. My father tried to save me, but they slapped him so hard he lost two teeth. It was on the second night of Hanukkah. The next day the captured boys were led into the synagogue to take an oath that they would serve the Tsar faithfully. Half the towns-people gathered before the synagogue. Men and women were

[77

crying, and in the crowd I saw Reizel. In all misery I managed to call out, 'Reizel, I will come back to you.' And she called back, 'Yankele, I will wait for you.'

"If I wanted to tell you what I went through, I could write a book of a thousand pages. They drove me somewhere deep into Russia. The trip lasted many weeks. They took me to a hamlet and put me in the custody of a peasant by the name of Ivan. Ivan had a wife and six children, and the whole family tried to make a Russian out of me. They all slept in one large bed. In the winter they kept their pigs in their hut. The place was swarming with roaches. I knew only a few Russian words. My fringed garment was taken away and my sidelocks were cut off. I had no choice but to eat unkosher food. In the first days I spat out the pig meat, but how long can a boy fast? For hundreds of miles around there was not a single Jew. They could force my body to do all kinds of things, but they could not make my soul forsake the faith of my fathers. I remembered a few prayers and benedictions by heart and kept on repeating them. I often spoke to myself when nobody was around so as not to forget the Yiddish language. In the summer Ivan sent me to pasture his goats. In later years I took care of his cows and horse. I would sit in the grass and talk to my parents, to my sister Leah, and to my brother Chaim, both younger than I, and also to Reizel. Though I was far away from them, I imagined that they heard me and answered me.

"Since I was captured on Hanukkah I decided to celebrate this feast even if it cost me my life. I had no Jewish calendar, but I recalled that Hanukkah comes about the time of Christmas—a little earlier or later. I would wake up and go outside in the middle of the night. Not far from the granary grew an old oak. Lightning had burned a large hole in its trunk. I crept inside, lit some kindling wood, and made the

benediction. If the peasant had caught me, he would have beaten me. But he slept like a bear.

"Years passed and I became a soldier. There was no old oak tree near the barracks, and you would be whipped for leaving the bunk bed and going outside without permission. But on some winter nights they sent me to guard an ammunition warehouse, and I always found an opportunity to light a candle and recite a prayer. Once, a Jewish soldier came to our barracks and brought with him a small prayer book. My joy at seeing the old familiar Hebrew letters cannot be described. I hid somewhere and recited all the prayers, those of the weekdays, the Sabbath, and the holidays. That soldier had already served out his term, and before he went home, he left me the prayer book as a gift. It was the greatest treasure of my life. I still carry it in my sack.

"Twenty-two years had passed since I was captured. The soldiers were supposed to have the right to send letters to their parents once a month, but since I wrote mine in Yiddish, they were never delivered, and I never received anything from them.

"One winter night, when it was my turn to stand watch at the warehouse, I lit two candles, and since there was no wind, I stuck them into the snow. According to my calculation it was Hanukkah. A soldier who stands watch is not allowed to sit down, and certainly not to fall asleep, but it was the middle of the night and nobody was there, so I squatted on the threshold of the warehouse to observe the two little flames burning brightly. I was tired after a difficult day of service and my eyelids closed. Soon I fell asleep. I was committing three sins against the Tsar at once. Suddenly I felt someone shaking my shoulder. I opened my eyes and saw my enemy, a vicious corporal by the name of Kapustin—tall, with broad shoulders, a curled mustache, and a thick red nose with purple veins from drinking. Usually he slept the whole night, but that night some demon made him come outside. When I saw that rascal by the light of the still-burning Hanukkah candles, I knew that this was my end. I would be court-martialed and sent to Siberia. I jumped up, grabbed my gun, and hit him over the head. He fell down and I started running. I ran until sunrise. I didn't know where my feet were carrying me. I had entered a thick forest and it seemed to have no end.

"For three days I ate nothing, and drank only melted snow. Then I came to a hamlet. In all these years I had saved some fifteen rubles from the few kopeks that a soldier receives as pay. I carried it in a little pouch on my chest. I bought myself a cotton-lined jacket, a pair of pants, and a cap. My soldier's uniform and the gun I threw into a stream. After weeks of wandering on foot, I came to railroad tracks. A freight train carrying logs and moving slowly was heading south. It had almost a hundred cars. I jumped on one of them. When the train approached a station, I jumped off in order not to be seen by the stationmaster. I could tell from signs along the way that we were heading toward St. Petersburg, the capital of Russia. At some stations the train stood for many hours, and I went into the town or village and begged for a slice of bread. The Russians had robbed me of my best years and I had the right to take some food from them. And so I arrived in Petersburg.

"There I found rich Jews, and when I told them of my predicament, they let me rest a few weeks and provided me with warm clothes and the fare to return to my hometown, Vitebsk. I had grown a beard and no one would have recognized me. Still, to come home to my family using my real name was dangerous because I would be arrested as a deserter.

"The train arrived in Vitebsk at dawn. The winter was about to end. The smell of spring was in the air. A few stations before Vitebsk Jewish passengers entered my car, and from their talk I learned that it was Purim. I remembered that on this holiday it was the custom for poor young men to put on masks and to disguise themselves as the silly King Ahasuerus, the righteous Mordecai, the cruel Haman, or his vicious wife, Zeresh. Toward evening they went from house to house singing songs and performing scenes from the book of Esther, and the people gave them a few groschen. I remained at the railroad station until late in the morning, and then I went into town and bought myself a mask of Haman with a high red triangular hat made of paper, as well as a paper sword. I was afraid that I might be recognized by some townspeople after all, and I did not want to shock my old parents with my sudden appearance. Since I was tired, I went to the poorhouse. The poorhouse warden asked me where I came from and I gave him the name of some faraway city. The poor and the sick had gotten chicken soup and challah from wealthy citizens. I ate a delicious meal—even a slice of cake—washed down by a glass of tea.

"After sunset I put on the mask of the wicked Haman, hung my paper sword at my side, and walked toward our old house. I opened the door and saw my parents. My father's beard had turned white over the years. My mother's face was shrunken and wrinkled. My brother Chaim and my sister Leah were not there. They must have gotten married and moved away.

"From my boyhood I remembered a song which the disguised Haman used to sing and I began to chant the words:

> *I am wicked Haman, the hero great,*
> *And Zeresh is my spiteful mate,*
> *On the King's horse ride I will,*
> *And all the Jews shall I kill.*

"I tried to continue, but a lump stuck in my throat and I could not utter another word. I heard my mother say, 'Here is Haman. Why didn't you bring Zeresh the shrew with you?' I made an effort to sing with a hoarse voice, and my father remarked, 'A great voice he has not, but he will get his two groschen anyhow.'

" 'Do you know what, Haman,' my mother said, 'take off your mask, sit down at the table, and eat the Purim repast with us.'

"I glanced at the table. Two thick candles were lit in silver candlesticks as in my young days. Everything looked familiar to me—the embroidered tablecloth, the carafe of wine. I had forgotten in cold Russia that oranges existed. But on the table there were some oranges, as well as mandelbread, a tray of sweet and sour fish, a double-braided challah, and a dish of poppy cakes. After some hesitation I took off my mask and sat down at the table. My mother looked at me and said, 'You must be from another town. Where do you come from?'

"I named a faraway city. 'What are you doing here in Vitebsk?' my father asked. 'Oh, I wander all over the world,' I answered. 'You still look like a young man. What is the purpose of becoming a wanderer at your age?' my father asked me. 'Don't ask him so many questions,' my mother said. 'Let him eat in peace. Go wash your hands.'

"I washed my hands with water from the copper pitcher of olden days and my mother handed me a towel and a knife to cut the challah. The handle was made of mother-of-pearl and embossed with the words 'Holy Sabbath.' Then she brought me a plate of kreplach filled with mincemeat. I asked my parents if they had children and my mother began to talk about my brother Chaim and my sister Leah. Both lived in other towns with their families. My parents didn't mention my name, but I could see my mother's upper lip trembling. Then she burst out crying, and my father reproached her, 'You are crying again? Today is a holiday.' 'I won't cry any more,' my mother apologized. My father handed her his handkerchief, and said to me, 'We had another son and he got lost like a stone in water.'

"In cheder I had studied the book of Genesis and the story of Joseph and his brothers. I wanted to cry out to my parents: 'I am your son.' But I was afraid that the surprise would cause my frail mother to faint. My father also looked exhausted. Gradually he began to tell me what happened on that Hanukkah night when the Cossacks captured his son Yankele. I asked, 'What happened to his bride-to-be?' and my father said, 'For years she refused to marry, hoping that our Yankele would return. Finally her parents persuaded her to get engaged again. She was about to be married when she caught typhoid fever and died.'

" 'She died from yearning for our Yankele,' my mother interjected. 'The day the murderous Cossacks captured him she began to pine away. She died with Yankele's name on her lips.'

"My mother again burst out crying, and my father said, 'Enough. According to the law, we should praise God for our misfortunes as well as for our good fortunes.'

"That night I gradually revealed to my parents who I was. First I told my father, and then he prepared my mother for the good news. After all the sobbing and kissing and embraces were over, we began to speak about my future. I could not stay at home under my real name. The police would have found out about me and arrested me. We decided that I could stay and live in the house only as a relative from some distant place. My parents were to introduce me as a nephew—a widower without children who came to live in their house after the loss of his wife. In a sense it was true. I had always thought of Reizel as my wife. I knew even then that I could never marry another woman. I assumed the name of Leibele instead of Yankele.

"And so it was. When the matchmakers heard that I was without a wife, they became busy with marriage propositions. However, I told them all that I loved my wife too much to exchange her for another woman. My parents were old and weak and they needed my care. For almost six years I remained at home. After four years my father died. My mother lived another two years, and then she also died and was buried beside him. A few times my brother and sister came to visit. Of course they learned who I really was, but they kept it a secret. These were the happiest years of my adult life. Every night when I went to sleep in a bed at home instead of a bunk bed in the barracks and every day when I went to pray in the synagogue, I thanked God for being rescued from the hands of the tyrants.

"After my parents' deaths I had no reason to remain in Vitebsk. I was thinking of learning a trade and settling down somewhere, but it made no sense to stay in one place all by myself. I began to wander from town to town. Wherever I went I stopped at the poorhouse and helped the poor and the sick. All my possessions are in this sack. As I told you, I still carry the prayer book that the soldier gave me some sixty-odd years ago, as well as my parents' Hanukkah lamp. Sometimes when I am on the road and feel especially down-hearted, I hide in a forest and light Hanukkah candles, even though it is not Hanukkah.

"At night, the moment I close my eyes, Reizel is with me. She is young and she wears the white silk bridal gown her parents had prepared for her trousseau. She pours oil into a magnificent Hanukkah lamp and I light the candles with a long torch. Sometimes the whole sky turns into an otherworldly Hanukkah lamp, with the stars as its lights. I told my dreams to a rabbi and he said, 'Love comes from the soul and souls radiate light.' I know that when my time comes, Reizel's soul will wait for me in Heaven. Well, it's time to go to sleep. Good night, a happy Hanukkah."